Miriam Steiner Aviezer

Dear Mary

AuthorHouse™ UK
1663 Liberty Drive
Bloomington, IN 47403 USA
www.authorhouse.co.uk
UK TFN: 0800 0148641 (Toll Free inside the UK)
UK Local: 02036 956322 (+44 20 3695 6322 from outside the UK)

Back cover image - Care Package, 1946-1947,
Paper and Cardboard - Stadtmuseum Hagen, Germany
Photographer: Heike Wippermann
Illustrations: Nogit Aviezer-Morag
Edited by: Nagham Abdulhai
Graphics by: niv-books
First printed in Israel by NIV Books Publishing

This book is printed on acid-free paper.

ISBN: 979-8-8230-8003-3 (sc)
ISBN: 979-8-8230-8310-2 (hc)
ISBN: 979-8-8230-8002-6 (e)

Print information available on the last page.

Published by AuthorHouse 06/05/2023

authorHOUSE

For my grandchildren,

Omer and Ariel Morag

Dear Mary,

Many years ago, I wrote you a letter that I have never sent. I am not sure if it makes sense to write you now, after all this time, but I thought about you often, and how I never thanked you for the package you have sent me; the package that have changed my life.

It was 1945, and The Second World War was over. People were coming home from camps, from their hiding places where they stayed for 6 years, hoping to find someone. Most of these people found no one, not even their home. Cemeteries were full and homes were empty.

A heavy cloud covered the sky and settled in everyone's heart.

At that time, I was in a recreation center for Jewish children who had survived the Holocaust. We lived in a big house with a huge garden filled with high trees, flowers, and green grass. Each had his own bed with white blankets, and we would dine in a big dining room with tables from wall to wall. We would wear nice new clothes and for hygienic reasons our heads were shaved and gentian marks were spread all over our heads and bodies. Without hair, our faces seemed smaller and our eyes bigger. We looked awful and we were very ugly.

I did not like to see myself in the mirror, or associate with anyone. I did not eat in the big dining room. I was allowed to take the meal to my hiding niche where I used to spend my time alone. I was happy when they just left me alone and did not force me to join them in their singing and dancing. There was not one single thing that could have moved me. Then, one day, I found a big package on my bed. I was not sure if it belonged to me, so I did not try to touch it.

Until Sister Klara approached me smiling and said:

"This is for you!"

I never received a package before. So I stood there, with my back to the wall, staring at the package the way you would stare at something that would jump the moment you touch it. Sister Klara tried to encourage me.

"Go on," she said. "Take it!"

Since I still did not do it, she took all the things out, put them on the bed and went away. When I was sure I was alone, I looked again at the things that were now laying on my bed. I touched them and took them one by one. I arranged them and watched silently. There was candy, chocolate, toys that were unknown to me, and a doll. I spent all that night only watching, touching, and smelling them, until I finally decided to use them.

I liked the doll the most.

She was not new, but that is why I liked her. Whoever sent it, must have done it with a heavy heart, for she was giving away something very dear to her. Something that was almost a part of her, and all that in order to please someone she did not know. The doll had blond hair, she could turn her head, close her eyes, and say "mama". she had a nice, red dress with white dots and lace panties. She only had one white shoe, for the other one was missing. And on the bare foot was written, with a child's handwriting:

Mary

Somehow, I knew that this was not the name of the doll, but of the girl who sent it. I closed my eyes and tried to imagine a girl of my age with blond hair, blue eyes, and a red dress with white dots, writing her name on the foot of her doll, kissing her goodbye and putting her in that big box.

This doll made a very long journey until she came to me. I took her in my arms and embraced her warmly, as though I had at last met a dear friend of mine. From that day on, I was not alone nor lonely. I had my doll which was special and mine alone, and I had a friend. It was you, Mary.

When I was putting the toys into the package, I remembered I was told it was a gift from 'The People of America'.

'The People of America!' It sounded so beautiful that I enjoyed repeating it, on and on, until it ceased to be a melody caressing my ears, and I began mumbling silently to myself:

"The People of America!"

I wondered how they look like, the People of America. Never had I met one, but as the time passed, I built a certain image of the Americans; Sympathetic and happy people, who like to laugh and tell jokes. They look chubby, and like to drink milk and eat ripe fruit and half-boiled vegetables.

They talk a lot on the telephone, and are always in a hurry. They have no secrets; they are like an open book; good people who are ready to share what they have with others. Even with an ugly child like me.

It appeared to me that I did not thank anyone for that wonderful gift, so I told Sister Klara that I would like to send a thank you letter for the package.

"To whom would you like to write?" she asked.

And I said, "to the People of America!"

She smiled, caressed my cheek and explained that one cannot write to a "People", and that I have to choose someone with a name and an address, and only then I could send the letter.

You, Mary, were the only person I "knew". In fact, in my eyes you were the People of America, and I wanted to write to you. Since I did not have the address, I did not send the letter. But

I was sure you existed, and that one day I will be able to thank you, the one who brought back the smile to my lips, and shared with me those unforgettable days, without even knowing it.

Many years had passed since, and you, Mary, probably have a big family with children and grand-children, just like me. I am sure that you have forgotten about the package you have sent me many years ago, with a blond-haired doll, with one shoe and the name "Mary" on the bare foot.

But I did not forget!

All those years, all I wanted was to write a letter and say:

Thank you, People of America!